THE MOVIE STORYBOOK

Printed in the United States of America

First Edition

1 3 5 7 9 10 8 6 4 2

This book is set in Romic Light 14 pt.

Library of Congress Catalog Card Number: 2005905552

ISBN: 1-4231-0025-5

Visit www.pirates.movies.com

DISNEY
PIRATES of the CARIBBEAN
DEAD MAN'S CHEST

THE MOVIE STORYBOOK

Adapted by Catherine McCafferty
Based on the screenplay written by Ted Elliott & Terry Rossio
Based on characters created by Ted Elliott & Terry Rossio
and Stuart Beattie and Jay Wolpert
Based on Walt Disney's Pirates of the Caribbean
Produced by Jerry Bruckheimer
Directed by Gore Verbinski

DISNEY PRESS
New York

Captain Jack Sparrow had cheated death once again. The legendary pirate had taken a treasure, escaped a Turkish prison, and returned to captain the *Black Pearl*.

His crew was not impressed with Jack's "treasure." It was not gold or jewels—it was an image of a key printed on a small piece of cloth.

"Captain, I think the crew—meaning me as well—we were expecting something a bit more . . . rewarding," said Gibbs, Jack's first mate.

"You're feeling that I'm not serving your interests as captain?" asked Jack.

"Abandon ship!" squawked the parrot that usually spoke only for the mute sailor, Cotton. This time he spoke for the entire crew—they were *not* happy with Jack!

Jack glared at the parrot and then gave his orders, "Set sail in a general . . . that way direction." Jack knew what he was doing. Mostly.

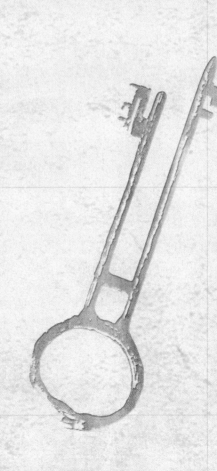

Far away, in Port Royal, Lord Cutler Beckett knew *exactly* what *he* was doing. First, he escorted Will Turner to his wedding in chains. Then, he also arrested the bride, Elizabeth Swann.

"And I have another warrant for Commodore James Norrington," added Beckett. "Any idea where he is?"

Elizabeth told him that Norrington had lost his post. But Elizabeth didn't want to talk about the commodore. She was more interested in what was happening here.

"What are the charges?" she demanded.

"The charge is conspiring to secure the unlawful release of a convict condemned to death. You do remember a certain pirate named Jack Sparrow?" Beckett asked.

"*Captain* Jack Sparrow," corrected Will and Elizabeth in unison.

Jack had crossed and doubled-crossed Elizabeth and Will into
helping him retrieve his ship, the *Black Pearl*. Oh, yes, they
remembered him. He was hard to forget.

Beckett sent them both off to prison. Later, Will was brought to
Beckett's office for a talk. On the wall, Will noticed a map of the world,

partly finished. On that same map, Beckett saw the many seas he wanted to control.

"The East India Trading Company has need of your services," said Beckett. Then he added, "I ask you to go to Captain Sparrow and recover a certain property in his possession."

Will did not believe Jack would just hand over his property if there was nothing in it for him. Jack would need a reward.

Beckett held out papers signed by the King of England. "These are Letters of Marque—a full pardon for Jack," he told Will. "The item in question is a compass Sparrow keeps with him at all times.

Bring back the Compass, or there's no deal."

Will had no choice. If he didn't do what Beckett wanted, he and Elizabeth would face the hangman's noose. He went to see Elizabeth in jail. "Tortuga," he told her. "I'll start there." Then he kissed her good-bye and set out to find Captain Jack Sparrow.

Elizabeth wasn't about to be left behind. With the help of her father and a loaded pistol, she escaped from prison and made her way to Beckett's office. Then she made her own deal with him. He signed and sealed the Letters of Marque that would guarantee Will's freedom. In return, Elizabeth told Beckett about the cursed chest of Aztec Gold that she thought he wanted.

But Beckett surprised her. "There is more than one chest of value in these waters," he said, gazing at the map.

Elizabeth wasn't sure what he meant, but she didn't wait to find out. It was time to find Will.

As Elizabeth tried to find Will and Will tried to find Jack, Jack tried to find a direction for his ship. Jack's Compass had never pointed north, but it had always pointed him in the direction he wanted to go. Until now.

Inside the *Black Pearl's* rum locker, Jack shook his Compass.

"Time's run out, Jack," a voice spoke from the shadows.

Jack turned to see a face from his past. "Bootstrap? Bill Turner?"

The spirit of Jack's old crewmate, and Will Turner's father, stepped forward. Years before, Bootstrap had spoken out against the mutinous Captain Barbossa, who had taken the *Black Pearl* from Jack for a time. Barbossa had sunk Bootstrap in the ocean's depths as punishment. To keep death away, Bootstrap had made a deal with the evil sea spirit, Davy Jones. Now Bootstrap was bound to serve Jones for one hundred years aboard Jones's ship, the *Flying Dutchman*.

"Davy Jones sent me as an emissary," said Bootstrap. "You made a deal with him, Jack. He raised the *Pearl* from the depths for you, and thirteen years you've been her captain. The terms what applied to me apply to you, as well. One soul, bound to crew a lifetime upon his ship."

"The *Flying Dutchman* already has a captain, so there's no need for me," Jack objected.

Bootstrap shook his head. "Jones's Kraken will find you and drag the *Pearl* back to the depths, and you along with it."

"Any idea when Jones will release said terrible beastie?" Jack asked.

Bootstrap pointed to Jack's hand. "I told you, Jack," he said, "your time is up."

As Bootstrap disappeared, the dreaded Black Spot appeared on Jack's hand. It meant he was a marked man. Jack stared at the spot of death, then shouted for his crew to make for land. Davy Jones and his sea beast couldn't follow him onto land, Jack reasoned. It was his only chance to get away.

Meanwhile, Will Turner had searched all over the islands for Jack Sparrow. "I heard he was dead," said a sunburned sailor on a dock.

On a ship, a fisherman told him: "Sure as the tide, Jack Sparrow will turn up in Singapore." While in Tortuga, Will got a slap on the face when he asked after Jack. No one had seen Jack anywhere.

Then, he found a shrimper in the shallows. "Can't say if Jack is there, but you'll find a ship on an island just south of the straights," the old man said. "A ship with black sails."

When Will Turner finally found Jack Sparrow, he was ruling over an island of fierce warriors. Captain Jack had become King Jack, and he was about to receive the greatest honor the islanders could bestow. They would make Jack a fine dinner—or rather, *into* a fine dinner!

"Save me," Jack hissed to Will.

Will managed to save Jack and some of his crew, and they once again set sail on the *Black Pearl*. Unfortunately, Will didn't know that Elizabeth was on her way to him. And Jack never mentioned that Davy Jones and his Kraken might be closing in, too.

When Will told Jack about Beckett's offer, the captain had an idea. He made a deal with Will. "I will trade you the Compass if you will recover for me—this." Jack showed Will the cloth with the key on it.

Will studied it. If he could trade the key for the Compass, it could save Elizabeth's life. "So you get my favor *and* the Letters of Marque?" he asked Jack.

"And you save fair damsel," Jack finished.

Now, Jack wasn't entirely sure where the key was. So as soon as Will agreed, they went to see someone who could tell them.

Jack, Will, and a few of the crew took longboats up the Pantano River. They were going to see the mystic Tia Dalma. She liked what she saw in Will. "You have a touch of destiny in you, William Turner," she said.

Will showed Tia Dalma the cloth and pointed to the key. "We're looking for this, and what it goes to."

"You know of Davy Jones?" Tia Dalma asked. "A great man of the sea until he ran afoul of a woman. The pain it caused him was too much to live with—but not enough to die. So he carved out his heart, locked it away in a chest, and hid the chest from the world. The key," she nodded toward the cloth, "he keeps with him at all times."

"So now all that is left is to slip aboard the *Flying Dutchman*, take the key, and then you can go back to Port Royal and save your bonnie lass," Jack said. He was ready to send Will on his way . . . and to get out of Tia Dalma's shack.

Tia Dalma stopped him. "Show me your hand."

After Jack showed her the Black Spot on his hand, Tia Dalma went to an upstairs room that whispered with the sound of ocean waves. She returned with a jar and scooped some dirt into it. "Davy Jones cannot step on land, but once every ten years . . ." Tia Dalma said. "Land is where you are safe, Jack Sparrow, and so you will carry land with you."

Then, with directions from Tia Dalma, they went to find Davy Jones.

Sooner than he would have liked, Will Turner found himself staring at a ship that Jack said was the *Flying Dutchman*.

"If you get captured, just say, 'Jack Sparrow sent me to settle his debt.' It might save your life," Jack told Will.

But Jack had tricked Will . . . again. Will rowed over to the ship, which was not the *Flying Dutchman* at all. Most of its crew was dead, and those living were hopeless and desperate. It was just the sort of doomed ship, Jack had known, that would catch Davy Jones's attention. Just as *Will* figured this out, the true *Flying Dutchman* appeared, with Davy Jones at its helm.

Davy Jones's eyes were cold, and his beard was made of octopus tentacles that twisted and curled. The pirate stared down at Will. "You are neither dead nor dying. What is your purpose here?"

"Jack Sparrow sent me to settle his debt," Will answered.

"Did he now?" Davy Jones asked. In that instant, Davy Jones disappeared from the doomed ship and reappeared before Jack Sparrow on the *Black Pearl*. "You have a debt to pay," he reminded Jack.

Jack pointed to the doomed ship. "You have my payment. One soul to serve on your ship. He is already over there."

"One soul is not the same as another," Davy Jones informed him.

Jack saw a chance to make a deal. "Just how many souls do you think my soul is worth?"

Davy Jones smiled. That was never a good sign. "One hundred
souls. I keep the boy. You owe me ninety-nine souls. In three days."

It wasn't one of Jack's better deals. But when he shook hands with
Davy Jones, the Black Spot disappeared. He was safe—for now.

There was only one place to get ninety-nine wretched souls to hand over to Davy Jones. Jack Sparrow turned the *Black Pearl* toward Tortuga.

One wretched soul Jack recruited was James Norrington, whose military career had been ruined by the wily captain. Another not-so-wretched soul was Elizabeth Swann. Elizabeth had disguised herself as a sailor and stowed away on a ship that had docked in Tortuga.

She confronted Jack.

"I know Will set out to find you," she told Jack. "Where is he?"

Jack gave her his version of the truth. "Darling, I am truly unhappy to have to tell you this . . . but through circumstances that have nothing whatsoever to do with me, poor Will was press-ganged into Davy Jones's crew."

"Do you have a way to save him?" Elizabeth asked, desperate.

"There is a chest—" Jack began.

"What contains the still-beating heart of Davy Jones, the source of his immortality," added one of Jack's crew helpfully.

Jack glared at his sailor and turned back to Elizabeth. "Whoever has that chest has the leverage to command Jones to do whatever he or she wants. Including saving our William from his grim fate." Jack waited. Sometimes, it was important not to rush a deal.

"How can we find it?" asked Elizabeth after a moment.

"With this." Jack brought out his Compass. "True enough, this Compass does not point north. It points to what you most want in this world." He carefully placed the Compass in Elizabeth's hands. "And what you want most in this world is to find the chest of Davy Jones, is it not?"

"To save Will," Elizabeth corrected.

"By finding the chest of Davy Jones." Jack opened the Compass. His deal was paying off. The needle swung and then held steady. The *Black Pearl* was underway—to *Isla Cruces*.

Meanwhile, aboard the *Flying Dutchman*, Will Turner had found his father. Bootstrap told Will about life on Davy Jones's ship. "You join the crew and think you've cheated the powers. But you lose what you were, bit by bit, till you end up like poor Wyvern there."

Will looked over at what he'd thought was a carving of a sailor. But this carving blinked and spoke! It was Wyvern. He had been a crewman for so long, he had become part of the ship!

"You must get away, Will," his father urged him.

"Not till l find this." Will pulled out the cloth. "Jack wanted it. Maybe it's a way out."

Suddenly, Wyvern moved. "The Dead Man's Chest!" Wyvern whispered. "Open it and stab the heart, and all are freed! But the *Dutchman* must have a living heart, or there is no captain! And if there is no captain, there is no one to have the key."

Wyvern's words confused Will. "The captain has the key?" he asked.

"I've said too much!" Frightened, Wyvern drew back.

But Will had heard enough. The key was close.

Will knew he had to act fast. When he saw a few of the sailors gambling, he joined in.

The sailors were wagering years of service on the boat. Will challenged Davy Jones for the key and won. Jones would not count Will as a part of his crew. But Will's father had gambled, and he had lost his chance to gain freedom from the *Dutchman*.

That night, as the sky met the sea in a curtain of darkness, Will found his father on deck. "Wait for me," Will said.

He crept to the ship's organ where Davy Jones had fallen asleep playing the instrument. Jones snored, but the tentacles of his beard were wide awake and alert.

When Will tried to take the key from Jones's neck, a tentacle from the captain's beard grabbed it back. Will tried again. This time, he held the key cloth out. The tentacle snatched away the cloth. While the tentacle was occupied, Will took the key from Davy Jones and hurried to the deck to get his dad.

"Come with me," Will said, as his father readied a longboat for escape.

"I'm part of the ship now, Will. I can't ever leave." Bootstrap pulled a black knife from his belt. "Take this. Always meant for you to have it."

"I will see you free of this prison. I promise you," Will said. "You are my father."

Bootstrap shoved his son away. He didn't want him to get hurt. "Do not come back onto this ship again."

Will silently repeated his promise as the longboat swung toward a passing ship. Will hopped on board. Now all he had to do was find Jack. But Jones woke up and discovered the missing key. He sent the Kraken to attack the ship Will was on. The Kraken destroyed it. Will's only choice now was to return to the *Flying Dutchman*. He knew that Davy Jones was after Jack, too. If he could stay hidden, he would have a free ride to *Isla Cruces* . . . and Jack's Compass.

Will reached *Isla Cruces* just as Norrington, Jack, and Elizabeth pulled the chest from the sand.

Norrington gaped at Jack as they heard the steady thump of Davy Jones's heart coming from inside. "You actually were telling the truth," the ex-commodore said.

Jack shrugged. "I do that a lot, and yet people are still surprised."

"With good reason," Will said as he moved forward with the key. Elizabeth gasped and rushed to greet him. "But I do owe you thanks, Jack. After you tricked me onto that ship to square your debt with Jones, I was reunited with my father." Will knelt by the chest and pulled out his father's knife.

It was Elizabeth's turn to gape at Jack. He had led Will to Davy Jones! "Everything you told me was a lie," she gasped.

Jack was less concerned with Elizabeth's feelings than with Will's actions. "What are you doing?" he asked.

"I'm going to kill Jones," Will told him.

The cold steel of Jack's sword pressed against Will's throat.

"I can't let you do that, William," said Jack. "If Jones is dead, then who's to call off the beastie?"

Will drew a sword. "I intend to free my father."

Norrington drew his sword as well. "I can't let you do that, either. Sorry. Lord Beckett desires the contents of that chest. I deliver, I get my life back."

The three swordsmen charged at once.

"Will, we can't let him get the chest. Trust me on this," Jack parried.

But Will wasn't about to trust Jack again. Or Norrington. In fact, none of them was about to trust either of the others. As their swords clashed, Pintel and Ragetti, a pair of Jack's even less-trustworthy crewmen, got an idea. They took the chest.

Elizabeth saw them sneaking off and raced after them. She reached the chest just as Davy Jones's crew reached the island.

At a break in the fighting, Jack found himself alone with the key and the chest. He opened the chest, removed the heart, and quickly wrapped it in his shirt. Then he hid it in the jar of dirt that Tia Dalma had given him. Jack set the jar in the longboat and closed the chest again. Norrington reached the longboat next.

Moments later, Davy Jones's crewmen had surrounded Jack and his crew.

"Get into the boat," Norrington told the others. He grabbed the chest and ran. Jones's crew took off after him.

Jack and the crew rowed quickly to the *Black Pearl*. Jack sat on the deck, waving to Davy Jones as the *Flying Dutchman* fell behind. "I have the heart. In here," he whispered to Gibbs and pointed to the jar.

Davy Jones gave up the chase as the *Pearl* pulled further ahead.

The beast at Jones's command—the Kraken—did not. The *Black Pearl* shuddered to a stop as it made contact with the sea monster.

Jack's jar toppled to the deck and smashed. Out spilled sand and dirt—but no heart. It was gone, and the Black Spot was back on Jack's hand.

Jack slipped onto a longboat to make for land.

Jack was halfway back to *Isla Cruces* when the needle of his Compass swung back to the *Pearl*. Jack whirled around.

Elizabeth was waiting for him when he got to his ship. She chained Jack to the mast of the *Pearl*. "It's after you, not us. It's the only way." She looked at Jack and saw that he actually admired her for doing what she had to do.

"Pirate," Jack complimented her.

Elizabeth joined the rest of the crew in their longboat, and they rowed away. The last time his crew saw him, Captain Jack Sparrow was slashing at the Kraken as he went down with his ship.

From aboard the *Flying Dutchman*, Bootstrap Bill also watched as the *Pearl* sank beneath the waves. He sighed sadly and the piece of his heart, untouched by the curse, broke a little. If there was one man who could have outwitted the Kraken, he thought, it would have been Jack.

Boostrap lowered his eyes. Captain Jack Sparrow was gone and the seas would never be the same.

THE END